Dora's Pirate Adventure

adapted by Leslie Valdes
based on the original teleplay by Chris Gifford
illustrated by Dave Aikins

SCHOLASTIC INC.

New York Toronto London Auckland Sydney
Mexico City New Delhi Hong Kong Buenos Aires

Based on the TV series *Dora the Explorer*® as seen on Nick Jr.®

ISBN 0-439-72386-8

12 11 10 9 8 7 6 5 4 3 2 1   5 6 7 8 9 10/0

Printed in the U.S.A.   23

First Scholastic printing, April 2005

Ahoy, mateys! I'm Dora. Do you want to be in our pirate play?
Great! Let's go put on our costumes!

Uh-oh. That sounds like pirates. Do you see pirates?

The Pirate Piggies are taking our costume chest! They think it's full of treasure.

If we don't get the costumes back, we can't dress up like pirates. And if we can't dress up like pirates, then we can't put on our pirate play.

We can get our costumes back. We just have to know where to go. Who do we ask for help when we don't know where to go? The Map!

Map says the Pirate Piggies took the treasure chest to Treasure Island. We have to sail across the Seven Seas and go under the Singing Bridge, and that's how we'll get to Treasure Island.

¡Fantástico! Now it's time to sail the Seven Seas. Let's count the Seven Seas together. *Uno, dos, tres, cuatro, cinco, seis, siete.*

Good counting!
Now we need to find the Singing Bridge. Where is the bridge?

The Singing Bridge sings silly songs.

Row, row, row your boat,
Gently down the stream,
Merrily, merrily,
merrily, merrily,
Life is but a
bowl of spaghetti!

We have to teach him the right words.
Let's sing the song the right way.

Row, row, row your boat,
Gently down the stream,
Merrily, merrily, merrily, merrily,
Life is but a dream!

Yay! We made it past the Singing Bridge! Next up is Treasure Island. Do you see Treasure Island? Yeah, there it is!

Look! There's a waterfall. Isa has to turn
the wheel, or we'll go over the edge.
Uh-oh! The wheel broke! Maybe Backpack
has something that will help us. Quick,
say "Backpack!"

We need something to fix the wheel. Do you see the sticky tape?
  Yeah, there it is! *¡Muy bien!*

Turn the wheel, Isa!
Whew! We made it past the waterfall.
Come on! Let's go to Treasure Island, and get our costumes back!

We found Treasure Island. Now let's look for the treasure chest. We can use Diego's spotting scope.

There it is! Come on, mateys, let's go get our costumes back!

The Pirate Piggies say they won't give us back our treasure.
We need your help. When I count to three, you need to say
"Give us back our treasure!" Ready? One, two, three:
Give us back our treasure!

It worked! *¡Muy bien!* The Pirate Piggies say we can have our treasure chest back!

Thanks for helping us get our costumes back. Now we can put on our pirate play. We did it! Hurray!